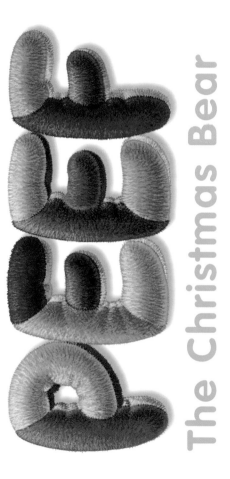

The Christmas Bear

by Tom Hegg

illustrated by Warren Hanson

Waldman House Press, Inc.

To Jimmy, who heard him first — T.H.

To my loving family, Patty, Cody & Lacey — W.H.

Waldman House Press, Inc.
525 North Third Street
Minneapolis, Minnesota 55401

Copyright © 1995, Tom Hegg & Warren Hanson
All Rights Reserved
ISBN: 0-931674-26-3
Printed in the United States of America
First Printing

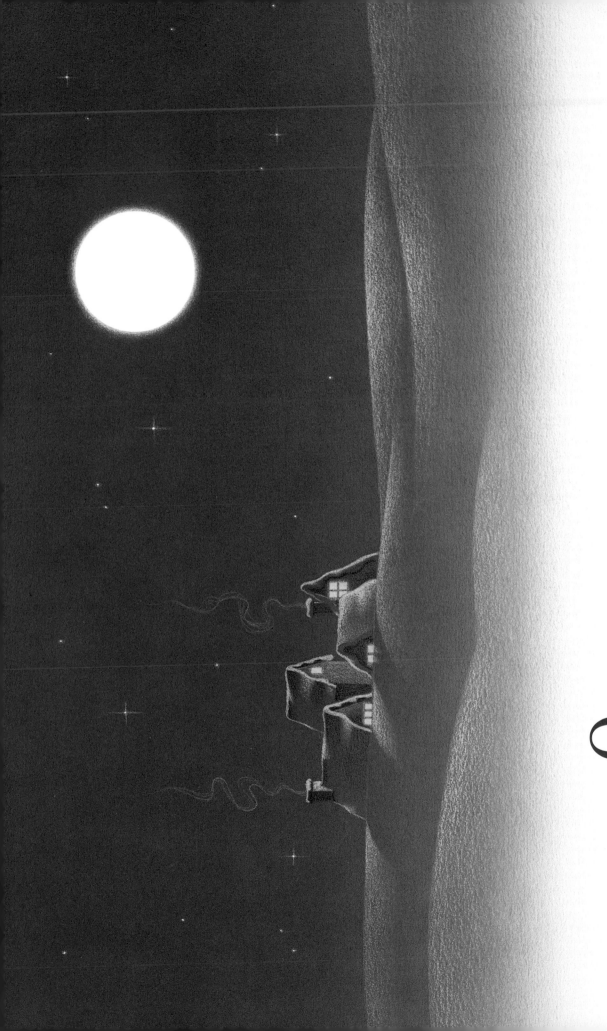

Once upon a polar night, so many years ago,

While starlight sparkled silently upon the hills of snow,

The elves in Santa's workshop heard a jolly, laughing call.

They put aside their work and made their way along the hall

To Santa Claus ... who said, "There is a job I need to do,

And I am going to need the help of every one of you.

Please bring a piece of cloth to me you prize above the rest."

They tried to guess at Santa's plan while walking to the chest

That held the bolts of fabric for the clothing and the toys

They made each year by Christmas for the world's girls and boys.

And every elf, as Santa asked, picked out one special piece ...

And brought it back to Santa Claus and placed it by the fleece

That Santa used for stuffing. Then, by golden candleglow,

They watched, with growing wonder, as the man began to sew.

A scrap of blue … a seam of pink … some green, some red, some brown …

Why, every color that there was was running up and down

The front and sides and underneath of what was forming there —

A Santa-hand-made masterpiece … a brand new Christmas bear!

And just before the last few stitches, as a final touch,

Dear Santa said, "A little bear who means so very much

Has got to have a way to say his name, now don't you think?"

The elves all nodded yes, then Santa Claus, quick as a wink,

Installed a little button in the tummy of the bear.

And then he said, "Now, all I need to do is touch once — there."

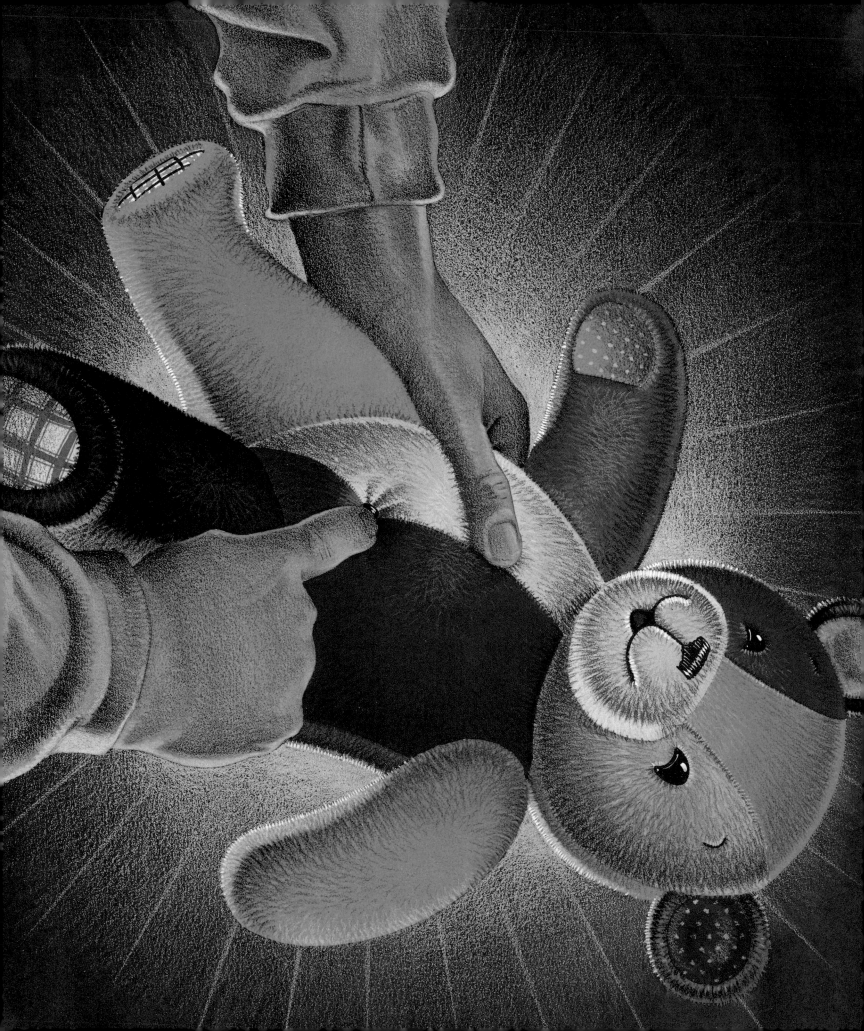

And as he did it, all the elves were stunned beyond belief.

The little bear had sprung to life and sung his name out — "PEEF!"

So Peef, the many-colored Christmas bear had come to be.

And how he'd ever done without him, Santa couldn't see.

For Peef became his chief assistant. Peef became his friend.

Peef would help to leaf through all the letters kids would send.

But when he read them, oftentimes his heart would feel a tug …

"Dear Santa Claus — Please send a teddy bear that I can hug."

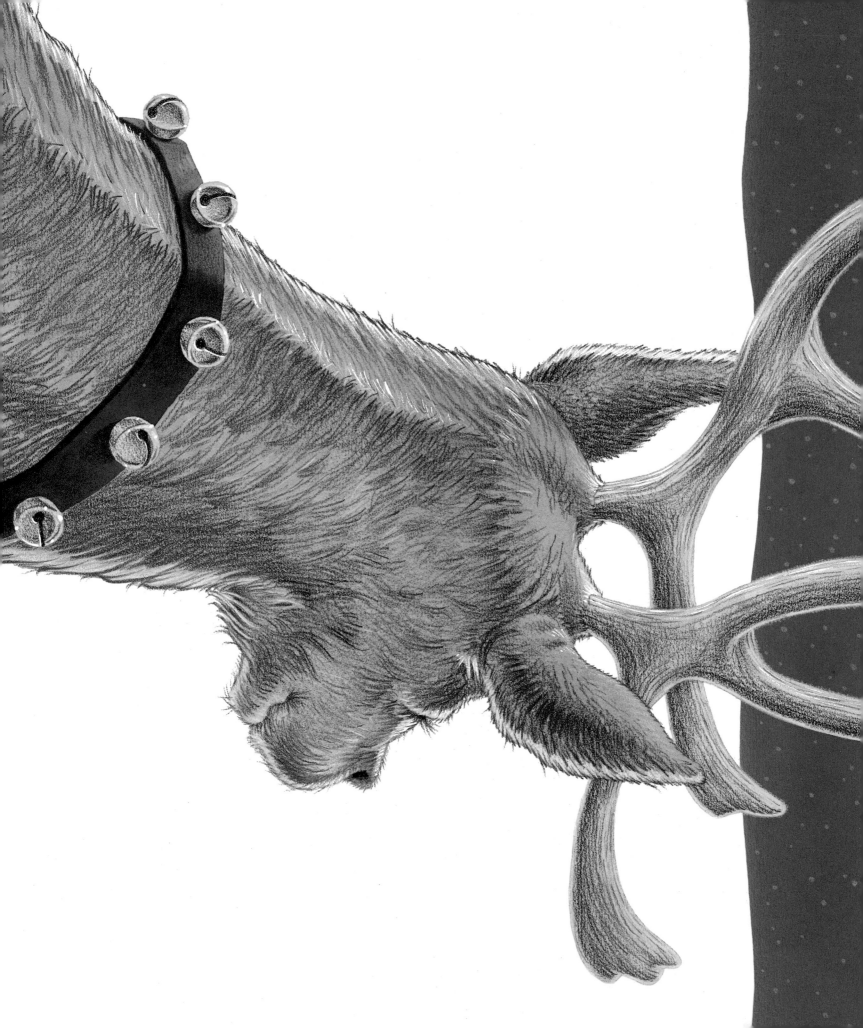

Peef loved his life with Santa. Oh! He gloried in the ride

He'd take in Santa's flying sleigh each year at Christmastide.

He played with all the reindeer ... fed them grain sheaf after sheaf.

They shook their harness bells as if to say, "Glad welcome, Peef!"

The elves would see themselves in him, and ask him how he was.

He'd peef with blushing thanks when they would praise his plushy fuzz.

For Peef, like all who lived with Santa in the polar cold,
Was ever new, and while he stayed, he never would grow old.

So Christmas after Christmas, Peef would climb up in the sleigh

And peef goodbye to all the toys that Santa gave away.

But sometimes, he would hear a piercing squeal of purest joy

And dream that he was in that magic first hug from a boy

Or girl who'd maybe dress him up … or ask him out to tea …

Or tell him all their worries in the pledge of secrecy.

Sometimes he'd steal a peefy peek into a frosted pane

And there he'd see a bear in bed, smeared red with candy cane.

And, Oh! He wished with every color of his very coat

That he belonged to someone who would sit him in a boat …

Who'd take him to the backyard and the blown-up wading pool …

Who'd try and try again to sneak him in with them to school.

His colors would grow brighter as the dream became more real.

He'd peef with sheer belief because he felt like he could feel.

But when the sleigh was empty, and the reindeer made for home,

That dream would end — like always — at the turn just north of Nome.

The days were very very busy (scarcely time for idle paws

Beside the barely-ever-stopping likes of Santa Claus!)

Peef peefed a happy melody that sweetened up the air.

Wherever he was working, Peef's bright bearitone was there.

And Peef was deeply grateful. Oh, he knew he had it made.

He owed so much to Santa! And that's why he was afraid

To tell the kindly man the truth. It seemed so hard because

It wasn't that he didn't love to be with Santa Claus . . .

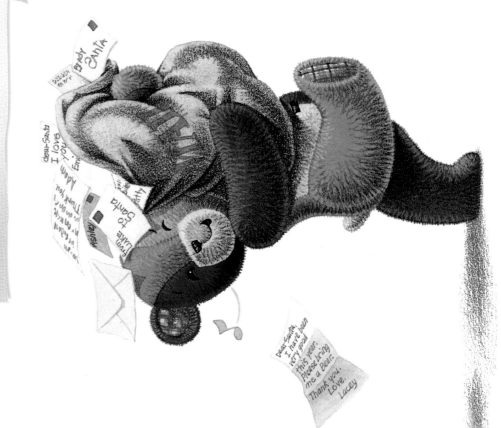

But still, no matter how he tried to hide his heart's desire,

He'd find himself with Santa sipping cocoa by the fire.

And as the burning logs would pop and hiss, he'd start to stare,

And there, within the flames he'd see a vision of a bear

Who looked just like him — lying right beside a sleeping child …

Exactly as a teddy bear was meant to do.

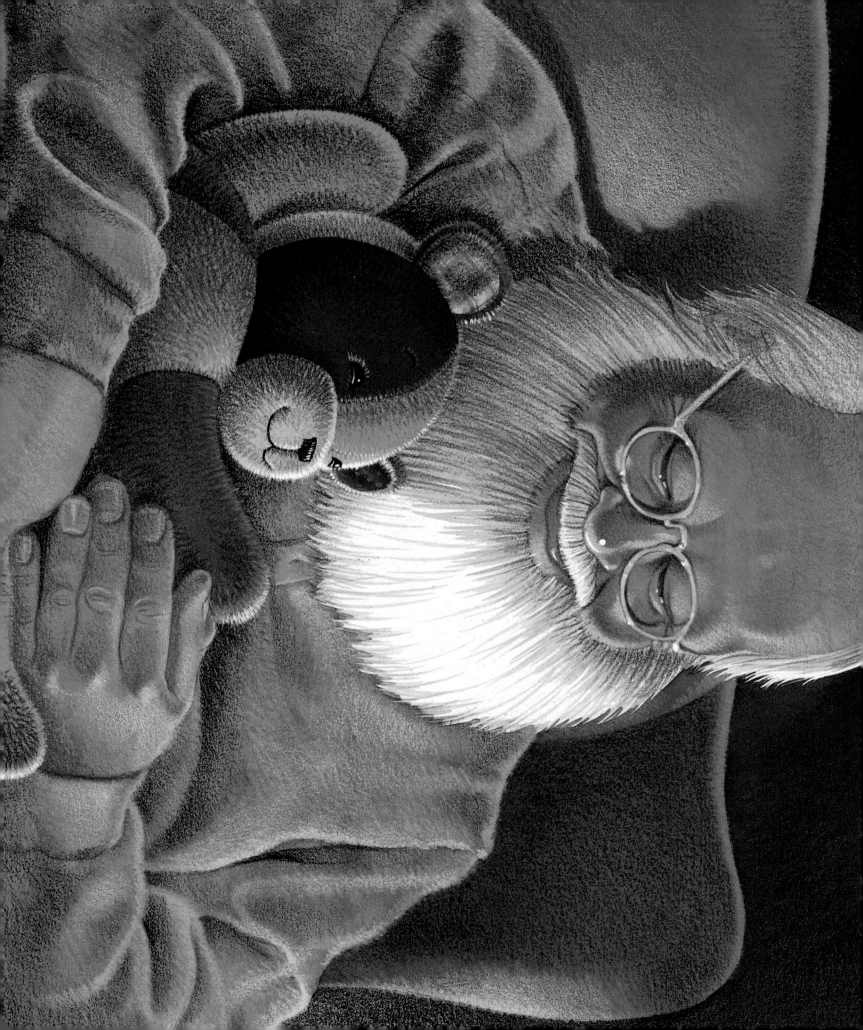

A wild excitement would go through him, and he'd jump in Santa's lap.

He'd almost say, "Please take me to the elves and let them wrap

Me up in Christmas paper. Let them take me to the sleigh.

Oh, Santa, how I love you, but you must give me away!"

But every time he tried, one breath before he'd had it said,

He stopped himself ... hugged Santa tightly ... then he went to bed.

And so, one year became the next … and Peef, the Christmas Bear

Remained at Santa's side, and never looked the worse for wear.

For passing time has no effect in Santa's magic land …

And tears repair themselves with just a touch of Santa's hand.

And jelly stains don't happen, nor do button eyes get lost …

And stuffing is replaced when needed, never mind the cost.

One Christmas Eve, while children dreamt of what was soon to be,

And Peef was dreaming back, "Oh, how I wish it could be me,"

He rode, as he had always done, right there by Santa's side.

They made their way around the Earth, with starlight as their guide.

And then, just as the reindeer turned to make again for home

Precisely at that old familiar turn just north of Nome,

The sleigh came to an altogether unexpected halt.

Why, Santa Claus had stopped it!

Then he said, "It's all my fault!

Now, Peef, how many years have I been doing this? A ton?

I can't believe I'm short of toys, and yet I am … by one."

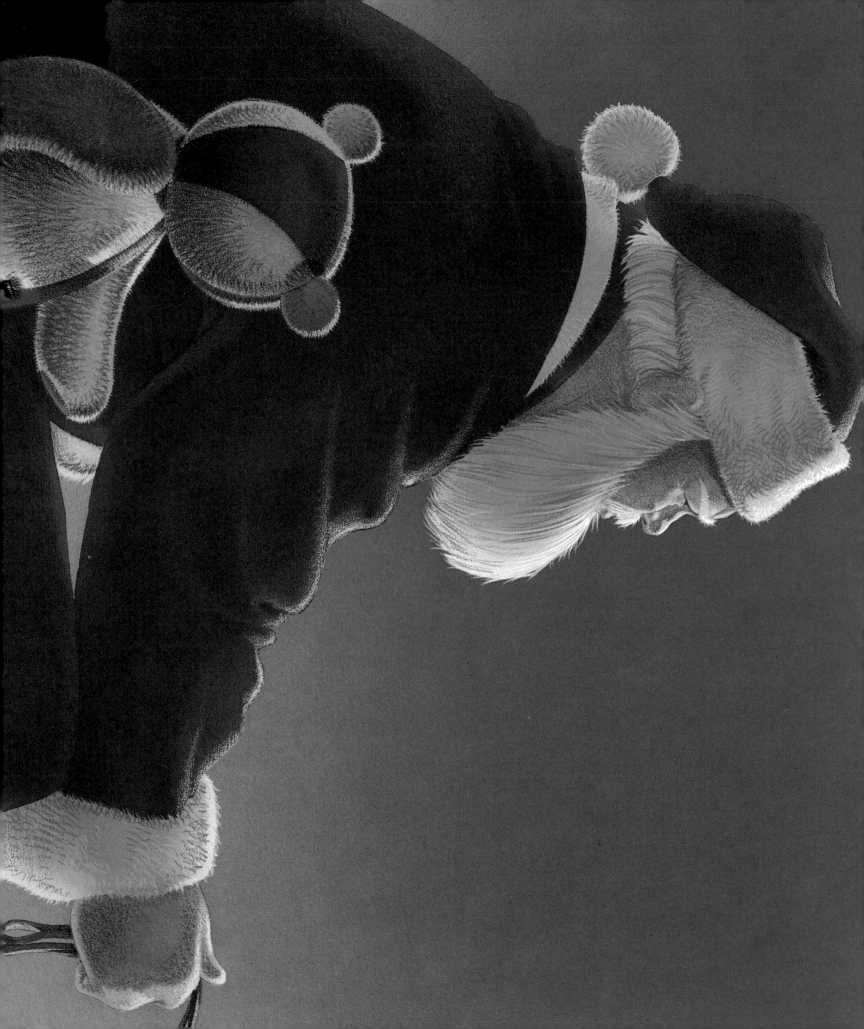

But there was something special in the tone of Santa's voice

That told the little bear that this mistake was made BY CHOICE!

And Peef looked up to Santa, but the old man looked ahead,

His eyes alight with … I'm not sure just what … then Santa said,

"We have a special duty to the children, you and I.

We can't forget a single one. You know the reasons why.

We have to think of them before we think about ourselves.

Besides, we have to set a good example for the elves.

I guess that what I'm trying to say …" Then he could say no more.

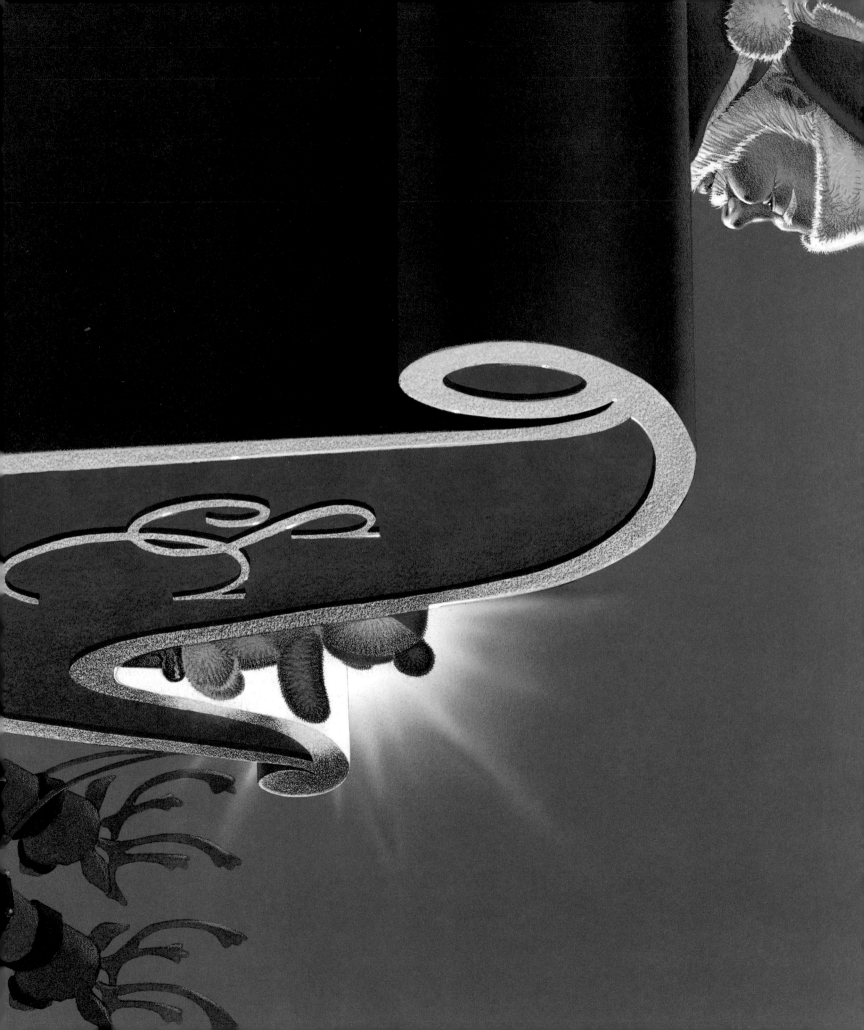

And for a little time, they sat together on the shore

Of Christmas day that washed the far horizon of the night.

And as the sleigh began to move again, a growing light

Began to glow against the inky canopy of sky …

Until a bright Aurora Bearialis filled the eye

Of heaven. Oh, the colors that adorned the Christmas air!

All radiating from the heart of one small teddy bear!

The little fellow peefed for joy. His dream was coming true.

For soon, a little girl or boy would say, "Peef, I love you!"

The sleigh alighted on a humble roof. Then Santa said,

"Say, little friend, you'd better trim your light. They're still in bed.

It's Christmas Eve. The neighborhood should still be fast asleep."

They stepped out on the drifted snow … so cold … so white … so deep.

Then Santa held the little bear he'd made so long ago

With bits of cloth from all the elves.

And then he said, "You know …"

But Peef's expression stopped his words, for Peef was well aware

That Santa wouldn't be around to fix each rip and tear.

Here, jelly stains do happen. Button eyes just might get lost.

But here's where he was meant to be, no matter what the cost.

And giving up that little bear he'd made with his own hands

From all the colors of the earth, in bright embracing bands,

Was how, upon one special night, with blessings from each elf,

That Santa Claus had given so completely of himself.

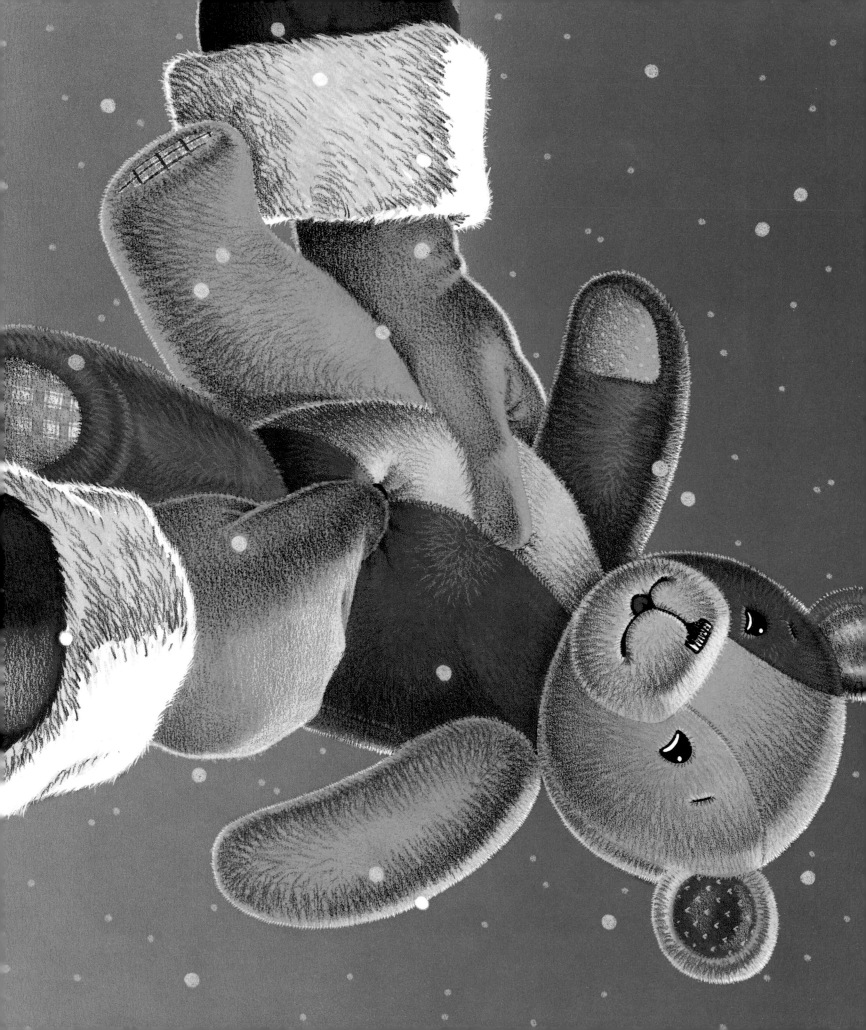

The little teddy bear made Santa smile from ear to ear

By saying with a twinkle, "I'll be seeing you next year!"

So Santa's finger pointed toward the tummy of the bear.

And then he said, "Now all I need to do is touch once … there!"

And as he vanished, one small child was thrilled beyond belief.

For right beside a pillow there, a little bear said, "Peef!"